BUTT OUT!

HEATH McKENZIE

FOR AVA & OSCAR–

butts out whenever and wherever possible!

First published in 2019 by Scholastic Press
An imprint of Scholastic Australia Pty Limited

First published in the UK in 2020 by Scholastic Children's Books
Euston House, 24 Eversholt Street
London NW1 1DB
A division of Scholastic Ltd
www.scholastic.co.uk

London ~ New York ~ Toronto ~ Sydney ~ Auckland
Mexico City ~ New Delhi ~ Hong Kong

Text and illustrations copyright © 2018 Heath McKenzie

ISBN 978 0702 30439 2

TODAY FEELS LIKE A GOOD DAY TO BE . . .

PANTS FREE!

Good HEAVENS!
Your BOTTOM is out!

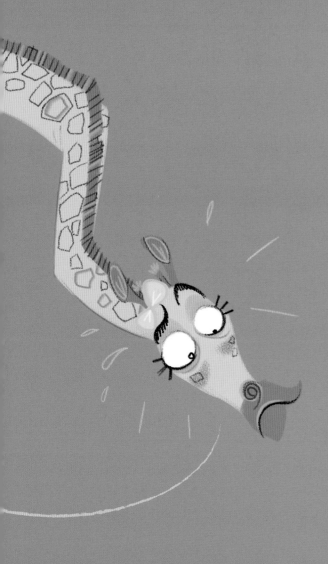

SUN'S OUT,
BUNS
OUT!

Excuse me, I do believe
you've forgotten your PANTS!

I DO BELIEVE I NEVER PUT ANY ON!

For the good of the children!
PLEASE put your BUTT away!

AND MISS THIS SUMMER BREEZE BETWEEN MY CHEEKS?

But . . .
but . . .
but . . .

YES, IT IS!

Hey, cut it OUT!

MORE LIKE,

BUTT

IT OUT.

I WOULD . . . .
BUT I
WON'T!

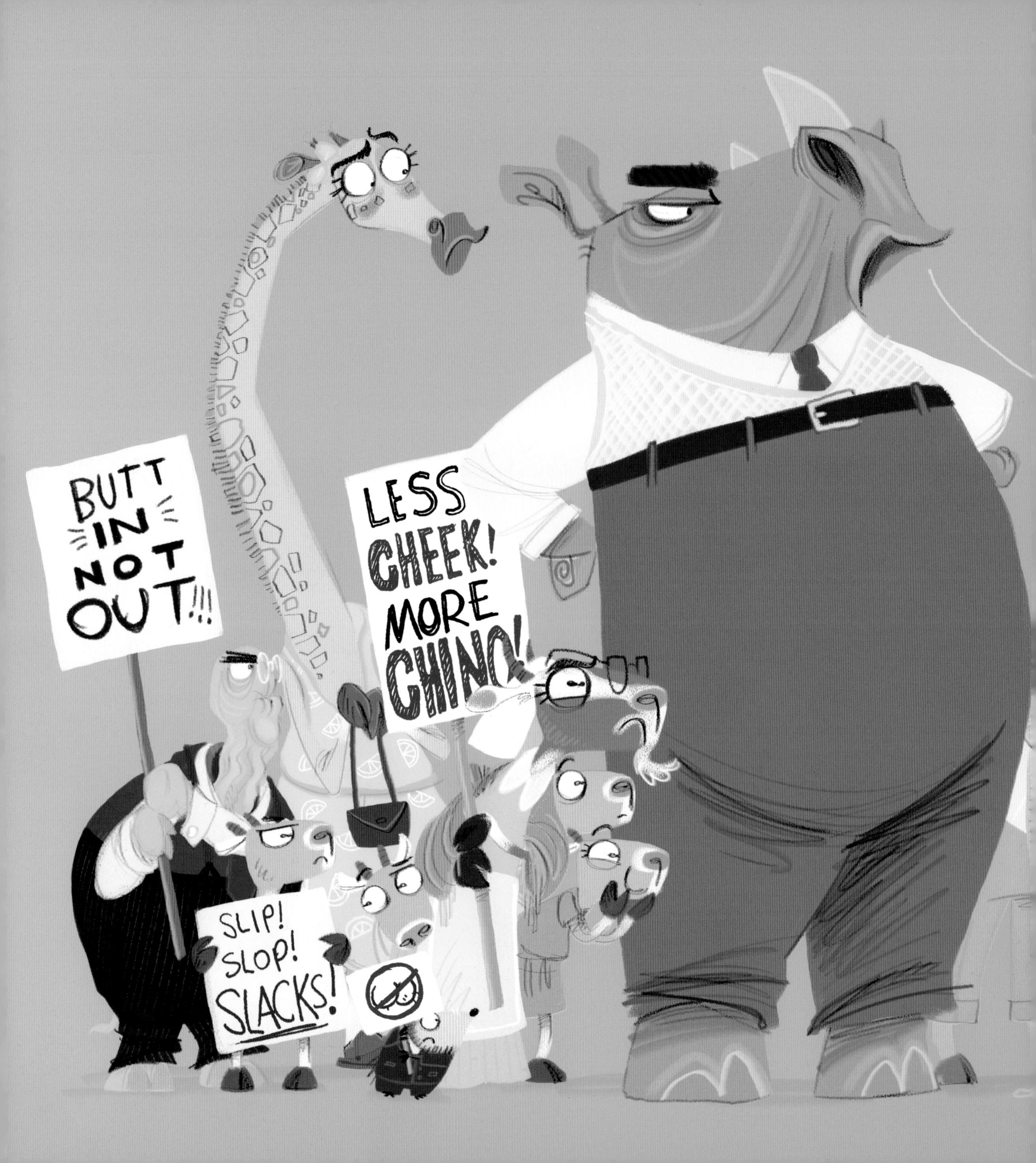
BUTT IN NOT OUT!!!
LESS CHEEK! MORE CHINO!
SLIP! SLOP! SLACKS!

RIGHT!

There is a time and a place for many things but now is NOT the time or place for bare bottoms, so can you PLEASE . . .

YES?

JUST PUT SOME PANTS ON!

FINE.

PANTS ARE ON!
NOW YOU CAN
ALL . . .

BUTT OUT!